Note from the creator of this journal:

Every person has something in them that is artistic and creative. This journal will motivate your inner artist and help you think outside the box.

# Open your mind, grab your marker, and be creative!

# Who am I?

FIRST NAME

_____

MIDDLE NAME

_____

LAST   NAME

_____

AGE

_____

# Color this page.

# THE

# ARTIST

# IN ME

# Finish the sentence below:

## Today is special because...

Today's date _____

# Write five words that describe you.

1.

2.

3.

4.

5.

# Using at least two words from the previous page, write two sentences about yourself.

1.

2.

# COLOR THIS PAGE YOUR FAVORITE COLOR.

# How Does Your Favorite Color Make You Feel?

# What is your favorite song?

Play your favorite song
and write how it makes

you feel.

# DRAW A PICTURE SHOWING HOW YOU FEEL TODAY.

**TODAY'S DATE**_____

# Write about how you feel today.

# IF YOU WERE A SUPER SHERO OR HERO, WHAT WOULD YOUR NAME BE AND WHY?

# WHAT COLORS WOULD YOUR SUPER SUIT BE? DRAW A PICTURE OF IT.

# What color is love to you?

If love was a food,
what would it be?
Draw a picture.

If love was a day of the week, what day would it be?

If love was an instrument,
what instrument would it be?

# If love was a scent, what scent would it be?

# What are you thankful for and why?

# If you could be an animal, what would you be and why?

# Draw a picture of how you would look as that animal.

# How does writing make you feel and why?

# CREATE A CHARACTER.

Give it a name:

Describe it:

Where does it live?

# DRAW A PiCTURE OF YOUR CHARACTER.

SiGN AND DATe _____

# Who or what makes you happy?

# Describe the perfect day.

Who is there:

What are you doing?

Where would you go?

# what do you want to be when you grow up and why?

Date_____

Finish this line:

It was a bright sunny day...

Close your eyes and imagine that it is
raining, thundering and lightning outside. How do you feel?

# IF YOU DID NOT HAVE INTERNET OR ELECTRONIC DEVICES FOR A WEEK WHAT WOULD YOU DO?

# Special Day

## What makes today special?

Today's date_____

# Did you enjoy your artist journal?

What did you like?




What did you dislike?




Today's date _____